MW00934146

FRANKINSCHOOL

To the TEACHERS
of Elmhurst (IL) District 205.
Your creative lesson plans and hard
work inspire kids—and parents too!

~ o ~

Also by Caryn Rivadeneira

Frankinschool Mystery #1: Monster Match
Frankinschool Mystery #3: Gone to the Dogs!
Helper Hounds: Penny Helps Portia Face Her Fears
Helper Hounds: Sparky Helps Mary Make New Friends
Helper Hounds: Noodle Helps Gabriel Say Goodbye
Helper Hounds: Robot Helps Max and Lily Deal with Bullies
Helper Hounds: King Tut Helps Ming Stay Weird
Helper Hounds: Spooky Helps Danny Tell the Truth
Helper Hounds: Brisket Helps Miryam with Online Learning
Helper Hounds: Louis Helps Ajani Fight Racism
Edward and Annie: A Penguin Adventure
Gritty and Graceful: 15 Inspiring Women of the Bible
Grit and Grace: Heroic Women of the Bible

FRANKINSCHOOL

The Cupsnake Escape

by Caryn Rivadeneira
illustrated by Dani Jones

RED
CHAIR
·PRESS·

Egremont, Massachusetts

RED CHAIR PRESS
BOOKS FOR YOUNG READERS

www.redchairpress.com
Free Discussion Guide Available online

Publisher's Cataloging-In-Publication Data
(Provided by Cassidy Cataloging Services, Inc.)

Names: Rivadeneira, Caryn Dahlstrand, author. | Jones, Dani, 1983-
  illustrator.

Title: Frankinschool. 2, The cupsnake escape / by Caryn Rivadeneira ;
  illustrated by Dani Jones.

Other Titles: Cupsnake escape

Description: Egremont, Massachusetts : Red Chair Press, [2024] | Interest age
  level: 007-010. | Summary: Fred and Luisa find themselves in trouble once
  again when the new student mixes up recipes at their class's bakery field trip
  leading to snakes running amok. While the students scramble out of the school
  in fear, Fred and Luisa suspect their old friend Frank is behind the Great
  Cupsnake Escape. Once again they put their creativity, their cooperation,
  and their courage to the test--but will it be enough to save the school from the
  snakes?--Publisher.

Identifiers: ISBN: 978-1-64371-301-4 (trade hardcover) | 978-1-64371-303-8 (multi-
  user ebook PDF S/L) | 978-1-64371-304-5 (ePub3 S&L) | 978-1-64371-305-2
  (ePub3 TR) | 978-1-64371-306-9 (Kf8)

Subjects: Creative writing--Juvenile fiction. | Monsters--Juvenile fiction. |
  Friendship--Juvenile fiction. | School field trips--Juvenile fiction. | Snakes-
  -Juvenile fiction. | CYAC: Creative writing--Fiction. | Monsters--Fiction.
  | Friendship--Fiction. | School field trips--Fiction. | Snakes--fiction. |
  LCGFT: Monster fiction. | BISAC: JUVENILE FICTION / Fantasy & Magic.
  | JUVENILE FICTION / Monsters. | JUVENILE FICTION / Social Themes /
  Friendship.

Classification: LCC: PZ7.1.R57627 Frc 2023 | DDC: [Fic]--dc23
LC record available at https://lccn.loc.gov/2022950228

Main body text set in Amasis Regular 17/27
Text copyright © Caryn Rivadeneira
Copyright © 2024 Red Chair Press LLC

Printed in Canada

1023 1P S24FN

MIX
Paper from
responsible sources
FSC
www.fsc.org   FSC® C016245

TABLE OF CONTENTS

CHAPTER 1:
IVY TOWERS

The school bus screeched to a stop. The walls and turrets of the high school loomed above the bus like a castle—or a fortress.

Ms. Martinez already told them they'd have to wait on the bus until all the teams arrived. Every year, the high school students offered a "clap in" to the Ook and Spook School Bake-Off teams as they arrived. Apparently, it was all part of the "fun."

Ugh. Fred's tummy rumbled with nerves

at the thought of it. All of it.

As the school's shadow poured over the bus, Fred shuddered.

"This school is so spooky," Fred said.

"Spooky?" Luisa said. "No way. It's *gorgeous*."

Fred rolled his eyes.

"Of course, you'd say that," Fred said. "Princesses *love* their castles."

"And of course you're scared," Luisa said. "Frankensteins *run from* theirs."

Fred cracked a smile as Luisa leaned over to peek out the window.

"I mean, look how the ivy creeps and crawls up the bricks," Luisa said. "And those weird windows! I wonder what's in *that* attic?"

Fred craned his neck to see the tiny windows at the top of the school's central tower. One window hung open—just slightly—on its hinges. Another sported a spiderweb crack across it. Another seemed covered by a sheer curtain—that suddenly moved. A body appeared and disappeared behind it as quickly as it arrived.

Fred jumped.

"Did you see that?" Fred asked.

"See what?" Drake said—popping up from the seat in front of them.

"It looked like, like—" Fred wanted to say *like someone peeking out*! But Fred already had enough to be nervous about today. The last thing he needed was to worry about people peeping out of a creepy school attic

tower. Finding a ghost and his laboratory in his own school's attic had been quite enough for one lifetime. So Fred just smiled at Drake and said, "Nothing. Just the ivy, I think."

And Fred tried to believe it. After all, Luisa had a point about the ivy. It was pretty cool. Fred rested his head against the bus window and followed a single strand of ivy up the bricks. It wasn't "gorgeous," but he did like how the twisted and tangled vines leaned in on each other. Like they were working together to climb the wall.

Except, one strand got higher than all the others. Not the one he followed, though. That one got tangled and lost in a mess of green. Dead leaves gathered in its vines as though the ivy had reached out and grabbed them. But another vine managed to sneak and creep ahead of the rest. Its tip waved and bobbed in the wind as the top of the vine tried to grip the wall—just below the window with the curtain.

Fred wondered why the ivy would want to be anywhere near that window—or this school.

In Fred's mind, there was nothing to love about this place. Not just because of the towering piles of bricks or the wings that spread on either side of the building. And not because of the *teenagers* who would be sure to point and giggle as they clapped while the baking teams weaved and ducked single file through the hallways.

No, the problem wasn't the *place* as much as the *reason*—even though it meant doing one of Fred's favorite things for Fred's favorite holiday.

Fred loved to bake—at home, with his dad. And Fred loved Halloween. Who doesn't?

But the Annual Ook and Spook School Bake-Off was something else altogether. For nearly forty years, the local elementary schools sent teams of bakers to the high school's vast cafeteria kitchen. There, each team would concoct their ookiest, spookiest recipe—created by the students themselves.

All that was fine. Great, actually.

The horrible part was that Fred's

grandmother *judged* the competition. In fact, Fred's grandmother *started* the competition.

Fred's grandparents opened Sigrid's Swedish Bakery not long after they came to America. The Ook and Spook School Bake-Off was a way to drum up business—and raise money for the schools. The winning students got a blue ribbon, fifty dollars, and their spooky creations sold in Sigrid's Swedish Bakery—right alongside the *limpa* bread, the *pepparkakar* cookies, the cardamom coffee cakes, and the fresh *bullar.*

The idea was a success from the get-go. It quickly became a tradition. Everyone loved it. Especially Fred.

That is, until this year.

This year, everything went *ugh.*

The moment the other students and parents heard that Sigrid's grandson had a spot on the team, they complained.

Kids shook their heads on the playground.

Dads posted angry rants on the town's social media pages.

Moms wrote letters to the editor of the town paper.

Grandparents gossiped on sidelines and in grocery lines.

This was unfair, they all had said.

All of it made Fred's stomach churn and gurgle. He wanted to quit.

"Ignore them," Fred's dad had said with a swoosh of a blue and yellow dishtowel. "My mother's tough—and fair. She let *me* lose the competition thirty years ago. Didn't you, Mom?"

Fred's grandmother had chuckled while her strong arms punched and pulled the *limpa* dough.

"You made a *terrible* cake. Absolutely disgusting!" she said. "I couldn't believe when I found out my own son—my flesh and blood—made that. Hmmmm... gives me an idea."

The next day, Fred's grandmother posted a newspaper clip about the day she gagged on her own son's cake. Under the clip she wrote: "Once upon a time, my son made a cake that nearly made me throw up. Thank goodness my grandson is a *good* baker. He won a spot on the team fair and square. And if he wins, it'll be fair and square just the same."

Then the principal reminded everyone that the judges did "blind" taste-testing—no one even knew who baked which desserts. After that, the town simmered down.

But Fred couldn't let it go. Every time he thought about the Ook and Spook School Bake-Off, every time he, Luisa, and Drake got together to work on their creation, his tummy rumbled. His palms got clammy. Because if he won, the rumors would start again.

Fred knew: the only way to stop the rumors, the only way to make sure no one accused him of cheating—or his grandmother of unfairness—would be to lose. But how could he make that happen?

His team's recipe was really delicious—and really spooky!

As Fred sat on the bus and studied the ivy, an idea came to him: Write a What-If Poem.

Ms. Martinez often had students write these to kill time—but also, to exercise their imaginations and "discover the power of pretend," she always said.

Last time he did this, Fred became Frankinschool—and Luisa became Princesa. They had met Frank the book-stealing ghost and saved the school from Frank's potions. Maybe it would work again.

Fred leaned forward and rummaged through his backpack. He grabbed his small notebook and a pencil and began to write.

What if I win?

Oh where to begin?

The town will be mad.

I will be sad.

I'll never show my face again.

But what if I lose?

If that's what I choose—uh—

we could make the snakes squirm,

like very small worms

That squirm on the head of Medusa.

Fredrik smiled. *Medusa*. That was good.
He kept scribbling.

We won't have to boast

that our cake scared the most.

We'll climb like ivy

Up into obscurity.

The rumors will disappear like a—

Fred's eyes darted up to the tiny window.
Something moved. As Fred looked up, the
curtain fell back into place. Fred felt his

neck and looked at his hands. No knobs.
Not green. But Fred had seen. Fred knew.

He finished his poem.

—ghost.

CHAPTER 2:
LONG WALKS DOWN MAGIC HALLS

"Single file, everyone!" Ms. Martinez said with a snap of her fingers. "Single file."

As they poured off the bus, Fred looked at the window. Of course, nothing. His mind was just playing tricks again. *Nerves.*

"Should we go over our plan again?" Drake asked. "I'm still worried the *fondant's* color isn't snakey enough."

"Good thing *vampire* snakes come in *lots*

of colors," Luisa said with a quick flash of her tongue.

"How about: no one knows what a 'vampire snake' even is so it doesn't matter," Drake said.

Drake—or "The New Kid" as most kids still called him—had come up with the idea of using *fondant* on cupcakes to create the "ook and spook" they needed for the contest. According to Drake, most people were already afraid of fondant because it had a fancy name. But, Drake told them, it's just like clay. They could turn the cupcakes into "Frankensteins and other stuff."

Luisa and Fred had stifled a laugh at this and suggested a different angle.

"What if we bake thin cakes and then

roll the fondant *around* them," Fred had suggested. "They could be cup*snakes!*"

"But is that ooky *or* spooky?" Luisa had asked. "Not everyone is scared of snakes, you know. How about we make them *vampire* snakes?"

"What the heck is a vampire snake?" Fred had said.

Luisa had thrust out her front "fangs."

"Like vampire bats. Except they're snakes. They've got big fangs in front— some speckled with diamonds. Like a grill."

Drake and Fred had rolled their eyes then. But somehow after several test-runs, the vampire cupsnakes turned out really well. They were delicious *and* spooky. Ms. Martinez thought they had a real shot at winning.

Fred sighed. Ms. Martinez was right. They did. At least, if they all cooperated—like the ivy—and stuck to their tasks, their snakes could emerge winners. Fred watched the other teams file off their buses. Some kids recognized Fred and began to point. Fred looked down. He wondered if they could ever guess he secretly hoped they would win.

"So?" Drake asked. "Should we go over our steps?"

Fred shook his head. "If we rethink things too much now, we'll just get more worried. And I'm already super nervous!"

"Nothing to be nervous about," Drake said. "Just because the whole town will hate you and think you're a cheater forever if you win…"

Luisa and Drake all laughed as they passed through the doors Ms. Martinez held open. Fred did not.

• • •

Ms. Martinez whistled and wiggled her fingers as the teams lined up inside the doors. "Stay with your team and follow me," Ms. Martinez said.

Drake, Luisa, and Fred clutched their supply bags and clustered together. The other teams scrambled behind. They stumbled forward as a push came from down the train of kids.

"Cheater," a kid hissed. "As if grandma's gonna let you lose."

Drake and Luisa turned around in a flash.

"Dunno," Luisa said. "Pretty sure your mom umped our softball game once. I remember her calling me out—and we lost."

The girl huffed, tossed her head, and turned back to her friends. Fred, Drake, and Luisa stifled their chuckles as Ms. Martinez motioned for everyone to follow her. As they tightened their bodies and wove their way through the serpentine hallways that led back to the high school's vast kitchen, the students clapped and cheered and gawked and murmured. Through it all, Luisa beamed.

"This place is the best," she said. "It's *magical!* So many secret stairs and passageways. Weird doors and small rooms. I can't wait to go to high school here and explore!"

Drake laughed. "I've been to four different schools—haven't found a magic one yet.

They're all as boring as the next. But I wish it *were* magic. I love a good adventure."

Fred hoped the school was magic too. If it were, once he got through this hallway— beyond the clapping, the gawking eyes, the pointed fingers, and the murmurs and got to baking, maybe his What-If Poem would do its thing.

CHAPTER 3:

GOOGLY EYES COME ALIVE

Fred wasn't sure what he expected from the kitchen, but it wasn't this. All around stainless-steel appliances *gleamed*. Deep sinks and broad countertops lined the walls, then curved into the room forming work stations. Grills, stovetops, ovens, warming racks, and shelved kitchen islands filled those spaces. Pans hung above the island, stacks of sheet pans rested under them, and rolling pins, utensils, mixing bowls, and mixers rested on them. Everything sparkled—ready to be used and dirtied.

And then, at the far end of the space was a simple table. The *judge's* table, where at the end of the afternoon, Fred's grandmother, along with the culinary arts teacher and a pastry chef from the next town over, would decide whose creation was the tastiest, the ookiest, and the spookiest.

"Wow," Drake said. "Maybe this place *is* magical!"

"Feels like we're on a cooking show," Luisa said as she imagined herself a Food Network television star.

"Well, I'm glad no one is filming us," Fred said. "My neighbor works at Channel 9. They'd probably say *that* was cheating too!"

Ms. Martinez snapped her fingers and began going over the ground rules. Each team had two hours to complete their dishes. She'd blow her whistle once halfway through—and twice at the end. Absolutely *no* talking between teams. Teachers would be on the lookout for raised hands if anyone needed anything. Bathroom breaks *were* allowed if needed—but hands must be washed for thirty seconds afterward followed with a good squirt of hand sanitizer. Does everyone understand?

Heads nodded to show they did.

"Alright," Ms. Martinez said, "I'll count down from ten. Then—and only then—can you unpack your supplies and start baking. Good luck!"

Ms. Martinez began her countdown: ten, nine, eight, seven, six, five, four, three, two....

"One! Spooky baking, everyone!" she said.

Suddenly the room was a flurry of motion: clashing pans, exploding bags of flour, thumping rolling pins, and scraping measuring cups.

Fred, Luisa, and Drake got right to work. Fred mixed the dry ingredients—sugar, flour, baking powder, baking soda, cocoa, and salt. Luisa measured the wet—milk, eggs, oil, vanilla, and red food coloring. Drake carefully folded the fondant and added drops of green and brown icing color. When the color looked snaky enough,

Drake began to roll out the fondant.

But as he rolled, the color dulled. Drake added a touch more green, a bit more yellow, and a dash more brown and folded again. Each time he rolled, however, the color went from vibrant to dull.

"Well, maybe vampire snakes are more like dull desert snakes than colorful jungle snakes," Drake said.

"It might brighten up while it bakes," Fred said as he turned on the mixer and watched the dry brown ingredients fold together with the shocking red of the wet ingredients.

Fred knew baking was just chemistry, that science explained the secrets of batter rising and color mixing. But still, Fred agreed with his grandmother who said baking was *alchemy*—the magical medieval process of turning one thing into another. That an oven could transform ingredients would never stop feeling miraculous to Fred.

Maybe Luisa was right. Maybe this place *was* magic. He could only hope.

As the cakes baked—and then cooled—Fred, Luisa, and Drake wiped and tidied their station. They cleaned their cutting boards, set the tiny "fangs," googly eyes, and tiny tongues in little bowls. They gathered paring knives for carving scales into the snakes.

Fred looked at the other stations. There, students topped cupcakes with licorice spiders. They spread white frosting on ghost-

shaped cookies and lined them with black. And they spread spun-sugar cobwebs on a gingerbread haunted house. Fred smiled at the cobwebs. Every year, somebody made a haunted mansion, but the spun-sugar webbing was a new twist. It might not be as creative as cupsnakes, but he knew his grandmother would love it.

If it tasted good, she'd pick the haunted house that's for sure! Phew. Fred didn't have to worry about the power of his pretending. Besides Drake was still unhappy with the color of the fondant for the snakes.

"Now it looks like poop!" Drake moaned. "That's not spooky—just gross!"

"Not much more we can do," Fred shrugged. "We don't have much time. We have to get cutting and rolling."

And so, they did. Luisa cut the thin cakes into snake-sized strips. Fred rolled the edges off the triangles into tubes. And Drake pressed the poop-colored fondant around each cake. Then they took turns pinching the heads and tales, twisting the bodies, and cutting tiny slits for scales, googels for eyes, and tiny sugar triangle teeth—some with rock-sugar diamonds, some without.

"Not *bad*," Luisa said, stepping back from their creations.

"But not *great*, either," Drake said.

Fred stifled a smile. The poop snakes looked *disgusting*. But he didn't say that. These cupsnakes were perfect for a party at the zoo's reptile house, but his grandmother would never choose them to win. She wanted to be scared, and these poopy guys—even with their vampire fangs—wouldn't scare anyone.

"They're perfect," Fred lied. "Let's plate them and bring them to the judges' table."

"Wait," Drake said—catching Fred's arm. "What's this?"

Drake picked up a gleaming bottle of green-and-gold baking sugar.

"Who brought this?" Luisa asked.

Fred shrugged and said, "Not me," but he secretly worried his dad snuck this into the supply kit.

"We can't use it," Luisa said. "It's not on our approved list of ingredients."

"What are you talking about?" Drake said. "This counts as icing color. This is perfect."

At that, Drake unscrewed the top and began to shake.

As he did, Fred shuddered and Luisa squealed.

As the glitter sifted down and landed on the cupsnakes, the snakes began to wriggle. Their tongues began to flick. Their googly eyes began to blink.

And children all around them began to scream.

CHAPTER 4:

THE RETURN OF FRANK

Licorice spiders wriggled off their cupcakes. Ghost cookies shook free of their cooling racks and wafted toward their bakers. Haunted gingerbread houses shook in place and a voice howled, "BEWARE!"

Then one by one, children and teachers buckled and fainted as a green mist wafted into the kitchen.

Fred clasped his hands to his neck. He stretched out his arms and picked up his feet. Sure enough, knobs sprung out of his neck. His skin tinged a green the snakes would envy. His feet grew heavy in his boots.

Fred and Luisa whipped their heads toward each other.

Fred stifled a smile, as though he had NO idea what was happening.

Luisa shook her wrists as the diamond bracelets returned.

"Yay!" Luisa said. "I missed these!" She pulled up her black gloves, tugged her riding jacket, and turned her heels to admire her boots. "And *these* are so much nicer than what I wear to ride horses at my Tia Antonia's farm."

They turned toward Drake, who stood

still. His mouth hung open. Four cupsnakes wriggled down from his scalp.

"Wh-wh-what's happening?" Drake asked.

"It's Frank," Fred said as he whipped his head around the kitchen to see if he could spot the culprit.

"Who?"

"Well, in a way *he's* Frank," Luisa said. "*Frankinschool.* And I'm Princesa Maria Luisa Octavia."

Princesa extended her gloved hand in a royal handshake.

"But Fred—er, Frankinschool—is talking about Frank the Ghost or Frank in the Attic," Luisa said. "He's behind this for sure."

"Did you say Frank the *ghost*?" Drake

said, brushing a cupsnake out of his eyes.

"It's a long story—a whole book really," Fred said. "And we don't have time to tell it right now. But clearly, Frank needs—er, *wants*—something."

Princesa flicked a flying ghost-cookie out of her face and asked, "But why is Frank *here*? I mean, he *just* got released from *our* school. Why would he come to *this* one?"

Frankinschool shrugged.

"No idea," he said. "We just need to find him—and fast. The last thing we need is to have to explain how a bunch of snakes and spiders and ghosts ended up all over the school."

Drake tugged at the snakes on his head. "I'm not so sure these guys want to slither

away anywhere." Then he smiled. "This is pretty cool."

Princesa grabbed a snake with her gloved hand and yanked.

"You're right," she said. "They're stuck!"

"Of course they are!" Frankinschool said. "He's Medusa—well, sort of. I don't think Medusa had *vampire* snakes on her head. But close enough!"

"What's a Medusa?" Drake asked. "And how did I become it?"

Princesa rolled her eyes and shook her head. "*Medusa's* not an 'it,' she's a *gorgon*—a monster, of sorts, from Greek mythology," Princesa said. "And she's amazing. Medusa got her snake hair as punishment, but I think it makes her more fierce and *fabulous*.

Anyway, Frankinschool here must've mentioned Medusa in a poem. That—combined with Frank the ghost's meddling—is how we end up in these messes. Ah, 'the power of pretend...'"

Frankinschool shrugged and nodded. "I didn't mean for *all* this to happen, though," Frankinschool said. "I just wanted our snakes to wriggle away and fall on the floor. Then they'd be too gross to enter the competition. And no one would accuse me of cheating!"

"You were going to throw the competition!" Drake said, twirling the snakes into a bun on top of his head. "We worked so hard. We *deserved* to win."

"I'm sorry," Frankinschool said. "But

you don't understand. All the teasing and accusing has *stunk*. I didn't want to go down in history as the Boy Who Cheated."

A snake escaped the bun and licked the inside of Drake's ears. "It's okay, I guess," Drake said. "You're lucky these snakes are so cool. Just don't call me Medusa."

"Well, we can still call you Drake," Princesa said. "But for the time being, you are Medusa. You should embrace her fierceness."

"I'll embrace my *own* fierceness," Drake said as the snake flicked its tongue up Drake's nose.

"Doesn't matter anyway," Frankinschool said. "We'll all be back to our normal selves soon enough. The snakes will be gone. Everything will go back to normal. I promise. We just need to find Frank."

"Do you think he's in the attic?" Princesa asked.

"He could be anywhere," Frankinschool said, flicking a licorice spider off his arm. "But I have a good guess."

"Maybe we should split up," Princesa said. "We don't have long until everyone wakes up."

"Split up?" Drake said. "Have you never seen a scary movie?"

"No, I'm not allowed to watch them," Princesa said. "My mom said they'll give me nightmares. But, still—"

"Uh, monsters?" Drake said. "We don't have to split up. I know where your ghost is."

The snakes on Drake's head untangled from their bun. They stiffened and flicked their tongues in the same direction. Drake pointed toward the back row of ovens.

"He's right there!"

CHAPTER 5:

SNAKE-CHARMING GREEN GLITTER

"Friends!" Frank said.

"What are you doing?" Princesa asked. "We *freed* you last time we saw you. Aren't you supposed to be in—you know—up there, out of limbo?"

Princesa pointed to the ceiling, where licorice spiders spun sugary webs that caught the floating cookie ghosts.

"You kidding me?" Frank said. "Being

able to float around town, visit my old janitor pals from the district *is* heaven. I'm having a blast—thanks to you two."

"Glad to hear it," Frankinschool said. "But you could've said hello without going through all this trouble!"

"You should talk," Frank said. "You helped create 'this trouble,' as you call it. And I need to thank you—you helped me solve the school's mouse problem."

Drake's hair-snakes started looking all around, searching for mice.

"Sorry about those," Frank said. "The snakes were supposed to all be *on* the ground—and heading for the vents. Not on your head. I'm not sure how *that* happened."

Frank shot a look at Frankinschool before

introducing himself to Drake.

Frank reached out his airy hand. Drake twisted and turned his hand as he tried to figure out how to shake Frank's.

"I'm Drake," he said. "These two say you have a plan?"

"Ah-ha! They hardly knew me but know me well," Frank laughed. "Of course, I have a plan! Those snakes are part of my plan—the solution actually, along with Frank's Magic Snake-Charming Green Glitter, patent-pending."

Frank leaned forward to pet one of the head-snakes but pulled back when it nipped his finger.

"Scary buggars, aren't they?" Frank said. "I hate snakes. But yes. The plan! Frank's Humane Pest Control. Could make me millions."

"What are you talking about?" Frankinschool asked. "Snake-charming patents? Ghosts can't get patents, and ghosts don't make money! Plus, you lived just fine with mice in the attic at our school."

"Is it proven that ghosts can't make millions? Maybe I'll be the first," Frank said. "And of course, *I'm* not afraid of mice, but these high schoolers sure are! And they've got mice running all through these halls, in the walls, in the stalls—ha! I'm a poet like you, Frankinschool!"

Frank slapped his knee, cleared his throat, and collected himself.

"But for real," Frank said. "The school's over-run with mice. Even in this kitchen. A real health-hazard, it is. Can't believe they let you bake in here, actually."

Frank stuck out his tongue and pretended to gag.

"But the janitors try to *poison* and *trap* the poor mice," Frank said. "I know what it's like to be trapped in a cage. I just want to help the little buggars. So I devised a plan—that might make me rich..."

Frank tapped his fingertips against each other and smiled.

"But you're *dead!*" Frankinschool said. "What can a ghost use money for?"

"Don't know," Frank said. "But I can't wait to find out!"

Princesa clapped her hands and let her diamond bracelets jingle at her wrists.

"I want to hear about it. I do," Princesa said. "But there are now mice *and* snakes *and* spiders *and* ghosts running amok—all over the school! We need to do something, fast!"

"Right," said Frank. "And *that* is a problem. I didn't know Frank's Magic Snake-Charming Green Glitter, patent-pending, would bring all the *other* things to life. But good news: I perfected the sleeping potion. Everyone in this place will be konked out until the bell rings. They won't notice a thing."

"But what about the competition?" Frankinschool said. "My *grandmother* is supposed to be here any minute now."

"You think I haven't thought of that?" Frank said. "Oh, shoot… Well, actually, I hadn't! What time are they coming?"

Frankinschool looked up at the clock. The second hand tick-tick-ticked past the twelve, making it exactly 1:30.

"The judging starts at 2:00," Frankinschool said. "We're supposed to be cleaning up and bringing our stuff to the judging table. If my grandma shows up and everybody *except us* is asleep, everyone's really going to think I'm a cheater!"

Frank waved his hand. Drake's head snake took another nip at it.

"Plenty of time!" Frank said. "Nothing to worry about. But, uh, about the cheating…"

"What about it?" Frankinschool said.

"I started those rumors."

"You did what?!" Frankinschool said.

"It was part of my plan to save the mice!" Frank said. "I can't wrangle snakes here on my own—so I planted a bug—er *snake*—in your ears and got to work. The *fondant* cupsnakes were my idea! Then I started the rumor hoping it would fire up *your* creativity. I needed one of your 'power of pretend' poems to get you back into Frankinschool form. Just in case I needed someone to scare the snakes who could then scare the mice—right out of the building. I'll admit I didn't see the Medusa thing coming. A new twist! Ah well, I can work with that."

Frankinschool sighed. It was nice that Frank wanted to help the mice, but did he have to make things so hard for Frankinschool in the meantime? No time to worry about that now.

Princesa pushed a roving snake away with her boot and asked, "But what do you want from us?"

Frank shook his head.

"From you and Frankinschool?" Frank said. "Actually nothing. You've already been very helpful. The plan is still to get rid of the mice—nicely. For that, I just need to borrow your new friend a minute."

And at that, Frank sprinkled Drake with Frank's Magic Snake-Charming Green Glitter, patent-pending, and whistled to the snakes on Drake's head.

"WooHoo!" Drake yelled as he and Frank vamoosed into the vents.

CHAPTER 6:

LOOKING FOR LABS

Above them, the vents rattled and mice skittered across them. Frank and Drake whooped and whooshed as they moved through.

"Are they actually having *fun?*" Princesa asked.

"Sounds like it," Frankinschool said.

He looked at the clock. 1:35. His grandmother was *always* early.

"We   don't   have   much   time,"

Frankinschool said.

"But what are we supposed to *do*?" Princesa asked. "How are we supposed to get rid of the snakes? And the spiders? And the ghosts?"

68

"Not sure," Frankinschool said. "But I know where we need to start."

Princesa and Frankinschool worked their way out of the kitchen, stepping over sleeping and snoring bakers and teachers and pushing their way through giant sugar-spun webs.

Once in the hallway, they looked both ways.

"This way," Frankinschool said. He lurched forward—hoping to run. But he forgot how heavy his Frankenboots were.

"Shuffle faster!" Princesa said as she galloped down the long hallway. Once again, as they peeked through classroom windows, students slouched snug and sleepy at their desks.

"It's almost peaceful—with the school like this," Frankinschool said.

"It won't be peaceful when they wake up to snakes and spiders!" Princesa said. "Look, there's the door to the tower stairwell."

Sure enough, just ahead the black door marked School Staff Only was tucked between rows of lockers.

Princesa looked both ways and grabbed the doorknob.

"Do you think it needs a key?" Frankinschool asked. "Or a code?"

He remembered the twisty-turning lock system from their school's attic door.

Princesa shrugged as she turned the knob. It gave—and the door opened smoothly and silently. No creaking as it opened to a well-lit staircase.

"Not spooky at all," Frankinschool said as they started their climb. At the top landing, they peeked out the windows.

"There's our bus!" Princesa said.

Frankinschool moved a sheer curtain out of the way and pressed his huge forehead against the window.

"Oh no!" he said as he spotted a boxy blue station wagon turning onto the school's long driveway. "There's my grandmother! We gotta hurry!"

Princesa grabbed the door handle at the top of the stairwell.

"Locked," she said.

Frankinschool crouched down in front of the door. The handle was smooth and worn—no signs of any secret code here either.

"I know this is where I saw Frank earlier," Frankinschool said. "He must have his lab up here."

Princesa tried the knob again. It didn't budge.

Frankinschool slumped down on the top step. "It's no use," he said. "The judges are here. They'll find out everyone's asleep. They'll see the snakes and spiders and ghosts. We might as well just go down and let them in. We can admit we cheated. I'll write a new poem. We'll change back. Being a *cheater* is better than being a *monster.*"

"Wait," Princesa said. "If you saw Frank *up* here, then you saw him *right here*. There are windows all around. The room behind us would only have windows facing the *other way*. And look: this window is loose on its hinges. That one has the cracks. And that's the same curtain."

Frank looked up and down, at the walls
and the landing. "But there's no lab here!"

"No lab," Princesa said. "But I have
another idea. Follow me."

Frankinschool and Princesa raced down
a flight of stairs.

"It must be here!" Princesa said as she
grabbed a door handle and pulled.

"What?" Frankinschool asked.

"The library!" Princesa said. "I saw the signs for the library on our way in. I remember thinking it was weird to have a library on the third floor."

And sure enough as Princesa pulled the door open, they stepped right between two tall stacks of books. Princesa raced forward and scanned the shelves.

"Just as I thought!" she said. "We're right in the *snakes* section."

"There's a *snake section* at the library?" Frankinschool asked with a shudder.

"There's an *everything* section at the library!" Princesa said. "That's what makes libraries magic."

Frankinschool rolled his eyes. Was there anything this girl didn't find magical? Then again, they were trying to round up cup*snakes* and chasing a ghost who had their Medusa-haired friend in the vent system. All based on a poem he wrote. Frankinschool smiled. She had a point.

Princesa pointed toward an empty space on the shelf and skirted off toward another area.

"Now we need to find the 'saints and legends' section!" Princesa said.

Buzzzzzzz. Buzzzzzz.

"Do you hear that?" Frankinschool said as he tilted his head toward the floor. "Sounds like a bell—a *door bell*. The judges are trying to buzz in."

"No problem," Princesa said. "I found it. I mean, I *didn't* find it—and that's what we need. Grab some paper and a pen—and let's go. I'll explain on the way."

Princesa pointed toward a student slouched across his table. His arms pillowed beneath his head. His notebooks lay scattered at the table's edges.

"He won't mind if you borrow a paper or two," Princesa said. "It's for a good cause!"

Frankinschool carefully tore two pages out of a notebook.

"I'll give them back. Promise!" he said as Princesa snagged a tiny pencil from near the card-catalog computer.

Frankinshool and Princesa burst open the library doors that led to the main hallway.

"The main stairs to the kitchen should be down here," Princesa said, rushing ahead.

Somewhere in the distance—down a different hall—they heard Frank and Drake whooping and hollering and mice skitter-scattering. All followed by a huge crash and more hooting and hollering.

"Look!" Frankinschool said, pointing toward a huge window at the end of the hallway.

"The stairs!" Princesa said. "Great."

"No. Look out the window!"

Princesa stopped dead in her tracks. Straight ahead, out the window, Frank floated and cheered—in the air beside Drake.

"Is Drake flying?" she asked. "Medusa

doesn't fly!"

"Looks like those snakes do!" Frankinschool said.

And sure enough, the snakes on Drake's head whirled like helicopter blades, holding him in place. Below them both, hundreds of mice spilled across the school sidewalk, into the street, and then toward the neighborhood just beyond.

Dogs barked. Birds darted. Neighbors screamed. But Frank and Drake continued to cheer and fist-bump, as best they could.

"Looks like they got rid of the mice," Frankinschool said. "But what about the other things?"

"That's what the paper's for," Princesa said. "We're gonna need another poem."

CHAPTER 7:
POWER OF PRETEND

"Another poem?" Frankinschool said. "Fine… uh… *The snakes turned back into regular cake… But it wasn't enough to save the day… Fred and Luisa and Drake lost… They went back home and no one gave a toss.*"

"Gave a *toss*?" Princesa said.

Frankinschool shrugged. "They say it on the murder mysteries my mom watches."

"Doesn't matter," Princesa said with a firm shake of her head. "Last time, we fixed this because of a weird old story, right? You used *that* to write a new poem."

Frankinschool nodded.

"Well, I began to wonder if *other* weird old stories weren't behind this too," Princesa said. "So I began to think about the stories we know about snakes and mice—well, rats. And I remembered what we learned about the Pied Piper in school—and what I learned about Saint Patrick at church."

"The guy with the shamrocks? What does he have to do with any of this?"

"It's not about shamrocks—it's about *snakes*," Princesa said. "Legend has it that he drove all the snakes out of Ireland. And the Pied Piper, well, he was hired to round up all the rats of this town in Germany. But the people wouldn't pay him—even after he got rid of the rats. So he played his pipe and the kids from the town all followed him too—just like the rats did."

Frankinschool stomped his frankenfoot.

"My grandmother—and the other judges—are right outside. We're about to be found out. Why are you telling me this?"

"Because," Princesa said. "This is the basis for Frank's theory. He combined these two stories—books on both are missing from the library—and came up with his idea to use *snakes* to drive out the mice. It's actually brilliant—and nice!"

"Okay," said Frankinschool. "But what does this have to do with my poems?"

Princesa grinned.

"Good thing you're already green," she said. "Because I think you need to become a Saint Patrick-Pied Piper. Saint Piper."

Frankinschool groaned.

"It's the only way to get rid of the snakes!" Princesa said.

Outside, Frank and Drake flipped and floated in the air. Drake grabbed a free-flowing strip of ivy and pulled himself toward the window. As he knocked on the window and waved frantically, Frankinschool said, "I think I have a better idea."

Frankinschool crouched against a locker and began to write.

What if—spiders eat ivy

And ghosts eat ivy

And snakes eat ivy too?

What if the ivy is sticky

And the vines get grabby,

What—oh what—would that do?

It would hold the creatures

While they revert

To their spooky-food form.

Then we'll pluck them out

Of all the places they're stuck

And avoid a ghosty swarm.

"What's a ghosty swarm?" Princesa
asked.

"I don't know," Frankinschool said.

"Doesn't matter. Let's see if they go for the ivy."

Frankinschool folded the poem and tucked it in his frankenpants while the judges buzzed the doorbell again and again.

Frankinschool and Princesa shuffled toward the broad windows ahead of them. They tugged and tugged until the window lifted. The wind blew the ivy vines right into the hallways. The smell of ivy permeated the halls, drawing the snakes, the spiders, and the ghosts like catnip. As the animals and ghosts began slithering, crawling, and wafting into the hallway, Frankinschool found himself whistling a lively tune.

"Sounds Irish," Princesa said.

Frankinschool shrugged. "Don't think so.

It's that song they played at the assembly," he said. "With those dancers from that foreign school."

"You mean those *Irish* dancers from the *Irish* dancing school?"

"Oh," Frankinschool said. "But look."

As Frankinschool shuffled and whistled, the snakes, spiders, and ghosts fell in line behind him. He stretched his arm out the window and the creatures followed. The ivy vines sprang up and wrapped the creatures in their tendrils. There, the spiders and ghosts stiffened and the snakes softened— all back to their original baked goodness. The smell of cookies and cake replaced the ivy as the cupsnakes, licorice spiders, and ghost cookies warmed in the sun. Once again, they looked good enough to eat.

"But how are we going to get them?" Princesa asked.

Frankinschool leaned out the window. He hadn't thought of that! He tried to reach an arm out to grab one—but it wouldn't reach. As the doorbell buzzed again below, Frankinschool was ready to give up.

They didn't have time to write another poem. It was all over.

That is, until Frank and Drake came somersaulting toward the window.

CHAPTER 8:

WINNERS AND LOSERS

"Need help?" Drake asked.

"The judges are here!" Frankinschool said. "We need to get the desserts back to the kitchen—and we need to wake everybody up. Fast! And of course, I'd rather not greet my grandmother in my Frankenoutfit!"

Frank saluted his friends and yelled, "On it!" as he disappeared into the building below.

A few of Drake's head-snakes stopped

whirling and formed a basket on his head. Drake floated and plucked the cupsnakes and spiders and ghosts out of the ivy and into the basket.

Princesa and Frankinschool ran back downstairs and into the kitchen—just as the class-dismissal bells began to ring. They ducked behind a row of ovens and shook as knobs sunk back into necks and diamond bracelets shimmered and broke apart, wafting into the air.

They hurried back to their station. Along the way they passed haunted gingerbread houses that made no sound. They spied licorice spiders that stood still and steady on top of cupcakes. And noticed ghost cookies without a sign of floatation.

Back at their station, the cupsnakes rested on their serving trays, with the right amount of cakey wiggle but the wrong shade of green. They still looked like poop on a plate with fangs and googly eyes.

A snake-less Drake snuck up behind them and smiled at his creations. "I don't know," he said. "They actually look pretty good. That is, if you don't know they've been either crawling on these gross floors or stuck on my head."

"Sssssssh!" Luisa said, but not before cracking a smile as Drake pretended to vomit.

Fred smiled at his teammates and took a deep breath. They'd done it. It was over. And from the look of their poopy vampire

cupsnakes, they probably *would* lose. All of this would be like a bad dream.

Except, this was no dream.

Fred, Luisa, and Drake walked their platters up to the judges' table and set them down. They followed the other kids back into the classroom where they'd wait for the results.

Outside, they could hear the high schoolers skittering through the hallways, yelling to one another as they went. But no screaming. This was good news. The snakes were gone.

The other teams yawned and stretched and wondered why the competition had made them so sleepy. Just all the hard work, they guessed.

Fred, Luisa, and Drake smiled at one another again.

"Frank is nice," Drake whispered. "We had a great time. And he was right! The snakes worked *perfectly* for getting rid of the mice. But the lady across the street probably wasn't too happy. About fifty mice ran *right* through her front door. Oops."

"Frank can drop off some brochures about his business now," Luisa laughed. "Maybe he will make a million."

As Fred began to wonder how a ghost could open a bank account, the door to the classroom swung open. The results were in.

The students reassembled in the kitchen, where Ms. Martinez stood with the high school pastry chef with an envelope.

"Well," Ms. Martinez said. "This has been *quite* the competition! We had an unfortunate incident—"

Fred's stomach dropped. He held his breath. Luisa gasped. Drake closed his eyes

and waited to hear.

"—in which one of our judges—Sigrid Johannson—became quite sick. Nearly fainted. She claimed she saw a *snake* slithering through the halls. She's fine now, but she thought her judging skills might not be up to the task. So, she suggested a replacement." Fred exhaled and relaxed.

"Turns out," Ms. Martinez continued, "Sigrid knows one of the janitors here. He used to clean their bakery and roll out their fondant when they needed it. Sigrid says Frank knows bakery goods through and through."

Fred's mouth fell open. "Frank knows my grandmother?!" he asked Drake and Luisa.

"Because Frank was so busy," Ms.

Martinez said. "Sigrid brought him a selection of each of your goods, and he sent down his choices—which turned out to be a tie-breaker!"

"Who's ready for the result?" Ms. Martinez asked.

The kitchen erupted into cheers.

"Third place: Licorice Spiders!"

Claps all around.

"Second place: Ghost Cookies!"

Claps all around.

"And first place goes to: Haunted Mansion with Spun-Sugar Spiderwebs!"

As Ms. Martinez thanked the competitors and the high school and then Sigrid's Swedish Bakery for hosting, all eyes turned toward Fred. Some kids snickered. Others actually looked like they felt sorry for him.

Fred didn't know how to feel. He wasn't sad about losing. He was confused about everything. Why didn't Frank mention that he knew his grandmother? And why wouldn't Frank pick their snakes? After all, he's the reason they made them.

But then Fred looked toward the judges' table. All the entries were still there— partly eaten, partly picked apart. But their cupsnakes were nowhere to be seen.

Fred smiled at Luisa and Drake.

"No cupsnakes on the table," Fred said.

Princesa pointed toward the kitchen window. Frank zipped in and out of the house across the street, wielding the cupsnakes as they chased out the mice.

"Looks like Frank is back in business," Princesa said.

"I hope he hires me again!" Drake said.

Fred laughed and looked up to see his grandmother walking toward him.

As she hugged him, she whispered: "I don't eat things that have been on the floor. Or on someone's head. Or in vents."

She kissed Fred on his head and said, "But I am having them come keep mice out of the bakery."

Then she winked and walked out.

EPILOGUE

Dear Fred:

Sorry that you lost. I'm sure they were delicious—although fondant is always too sweet if you ask me. And really...**fondant** in a school competition?!

Anyway, the cupsnakes are doing well. And the mice are much happier. We're working on driving the mice out into the forest preserves. Exhausting for the snakes, but good exercise. The fondant means they've got a lot of sugar to burn off.

Sorry I didn't mention that I know your grandmother. In fairness, I had no idea she was your grandmother until after you freed me from the school. I went back to visit her—and she told me all about her beloved grandson, Fred. Small world.

Imagine me again some time in a "What-If" story.

Your friend,
Frank, in the Attic

ABOUT THE AUTHOR

Caryn Rivadeneira has spent her life imagining what's up every roped-off twisty staircase, what's behind every creaky, sneaky door, and what's lurking in every spooky space she's ever passed (and it's possible she even snuck into a few of these places!). Caryn is the author of more than 20 books for children and grown-ups, including *Edward and Annie: A Penguin Adventure* (Tommy Nelson) and the award-winning *Helper Hounds* series (Red Chair Press). Caryn lives in the near-west suburbs of Chicago with her husband, three kids, and her rescued pit bulls. There may or may not be snakes in her kitchen.

ABOUT THE ILLUSTRATOR

Dani Jones is an artist, writer, children's book illustrator, and comics creator living in New Hampshire. Dani is the illustrator of the *New York Times* bestselling PopularMMOs graphic novel series from HarperCollins and creator of the picture book *Monsters Vs. Kittens* from Stan Lee's Kids Universe. You can learn more about her and her work at danijones.com.

IF YOU ENJOYED THE CUPSNAKE ESCAPE, READ MORE OF FRANKINSCHOOL AND HIS FRIENDS WITH BOOK 1: MONSTER MATCH.

Fred is working on his writing assignment when a strange green mist fills the classroom, and the words on his page come to life, literally.

Suddenly Fred—now Frankinschool—and Luisa— now Princesa Luisa—need to save the school from the mysterious potion—and the even more mysterious and devious ghost living in the school attic.

Ask at your favorite library or bookstore for **Frankinschool Book 1: Monster Match** and **Frankinschool Book 3: Gone to the Dogs.**